T0113820

FOR THE LOVE OF POINDEXTER

Othello Leneer Graham

"A 4.0 - GPA AUTHOR" GEM

authorHOUSE®

AuthorHouse™
1663 Liberty Drive
Bloomington, IN 47403
www.authorhouse.com
Phone: 1 (800) 839-8640

Published by AuthorHouse 04/28/2016

ISBN: 978-1-5246-0328-1 (sc)
ISBN: 978-1-5246-0327-4 (e)

Library of Congress Control Number: 2016905906

Print information available on the last page.

This book is printed on acid-free paper.

SNAPSHOT

A cheating boyfriend leads to Opal's devastation and restoration.

A Note To My Readers:

Please pardon any remaining grammatical, punctuation and/or typographical errors. I attempted to perfect, but may have fallen short.

GRATITUDE

To God, My Mother, Grandmother
and Uncle who are in Heaven.

To my Aunts... Long live the "Elephant"
(Doris) and "Duck" (Laura).

To all my Ancestors who shed their
blood in place of mine.

EMAIL

emailmeog@yahoo.com

1

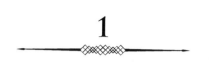

"I wonder what's keeping Daquan. He should have called me hours ago," anxiously thought Opal. "Maybe I should have warned him I was arriving back in town a day earlier due to the guest speaker becoming ill. Better yet, I think I'll just surprise my "boo" by showing up at his place with my most sexy Victoria Secret's lingerie." This time I will make his toes *curl*', pondered Opal. "Cabbie, take me to Brooklyn… I'll explain the rest when we get there," instructed Opal. "Yes Ma'am," responded the Cabbie. Once they arrived at Opal's condo, she instructed the Cabbie to wait for her to return once she had put away her luggage and changed clothing. Opal returns to the cab with a long trench coat, and an impish smile beaming from her face. "Alright Cabbie, take me to…, I have an appointment with destiny this evening." The cabbie gingerly transports Opal to her desired destination. "OK, Miss… we're here," stated the taxi driver. "What do I owe ya?" "Forty-one thirteen." "Here's a fifty… keep the change." "Thanks lady, you can call on me anytime!," happily remarked the cabbie. Opal proceeds to exit the cab, and head towards her boyfriend's apartment.

"This is almost like Christmas. I can't wait for Daquan to *unwrap this package*," thinks Opal. Opal is so anxious, she nervously fumbles to locate Daquan's door key upon her key ring. Opal quietly opens Daquan's apartment door, and tip-toes towards his bedroom. She hears sexy, lovemaking music in Daquan's bedroom as if he was expecting her arrival. Opal not being able to contain her enthusiasm any longer, bursts into the bedroom; flings her trench coat, and yells, "Give it to me baby!"

Daquan turns his head around, nearly having a heart attack! Another voice pulls back the covers and shouts, "Who is this bitch?!" Opal is aghast and utterly speechless when she witnesses another *"man"* naked in her boyfriend's bed! "What da **** is this ****?" shouts Opal in painful tears. "Um, Um, Um, I can explain baby," stutters Daquan. "Your trifling ass ain't shit! The last time I caught you cheating you were with my cousin Meeka! I can't believe your dog ass is *"gay"*"! I forgave you then by listening to your bullshit explanation to forgive your behavior and I did!" Responding with arrogance, "Well, if you wanna get technical about it; I'm actually *"Bi-sexual"*, answered Daquan. "But this time, your ass is grass!" "You are so right baby, he is grass, and I have manicured every delicious part of this fine man! He is just like Kentucky Fried Chicken girl… finger lickin' good!" "Time for you to *go* now "boo-boo", and time for him to *'cum'*, if you know what I mean", giggles Le'Fonz while degrading Opal." "Damn right Le'Fonz, we get down 100!" Opal removes Daquan's key from her key ring, throws it at him, and runs out of his apartment with absolute betrayal/disgust coursing through her veins.

2

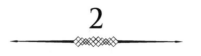

(Opal hails another taxi home while proceeding to cry and moan intensely.)

The next morning, Opal phones her Nursing Supervisor, and informs her she will be out for the next 2 days due to a personal crisis. Sharon (The Nursing Supervisor) reads between the lines by using her female intuition. She and Opal are friends/confidants. Opal spends the next 2 days pondering her future, and her past mistakes with men; especially Daquan. Then suddenly a frightening thought entered her mind. "Oh God, Oh God, please don't let me have *HIV*, or *AIDS* as a result of having sex with a bi-sexual man. Please God I am begging you. If you can forgive me, and keep me healthy to a ripe old age, I will serve you... I promise," pleads Opal. "If anyone should have known better to have unprotected sex; it was me. I am a Nurse after all." As time passes, Opal continues her plight by bargaining with God; mottling through. "God I beg you to send me a descent and Godly man. One who is after your own heart. In Jesus name I pray; Amen."

(Weeks fade into months.) (Opal and Sharon eat lunch at the Street Café.)

"How you holdin' up girl?" asks Sharon (Opal's immediate Nursing Supervisor). "I'm doin'", Opal remarks in continued anguish. "It's so hard to believe that Daquan was *gay*." "No offense, but that brother was the finest boy in school. I remember when you and I were cheerleaders, and Daquan took his shirt off to pose for a newspaper article. All the girls thought that he was sooooo fine, and too gorgeous. He was tall, muscular, dark and appeared to be *"packin'"* a donkey stick, if you know what I mean." "He appeared to be the perfect ladies' man. "A real *'man's, 'man'* more like it", harps Opal. What a waste." "Yeh girl… I know what you mean. He was a *man's man.* **He liked the holes and the poles.**" "I was caught up in the same spell of his physical charms. The old adage of *"All that glitters ain't gold"* is so damn true. I have indeed learned my lesson with that Nigga", assures Opal. "Well, girl it looks like lunchtime is over already." "Darn sure is", agrees Sharon. "We'll chat later" the girls say as they part ways both leaving a $5 tip for the waiter. The two depart the café across the street as they head back to the public clinic.

3

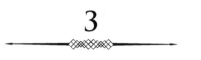

(Opal's next patient waits in an overcrowded lobby.)

"Morgan Chandler", calls Opal. "Please follow me back to your exam room Ms. Chandler. "It's Mrs.", corrected Morgan. "Alright. What brings you to see us today?" "Well, I am so embarrassed and ashamed. My parents don't know what's going on with me, nor do they know I am here." replied Morgan. "I see." "Mrs. Chandler, please pardon my forwardness, but you don't look like you belong on this side of town. Your Rolex watch, Gucci bag and the Lexus I saw you drove up in suggests wealth; being from the opposite side of these tracks." explains Opal. "You're right. I can't afford to be seen at the Doctor's in my area because people would talk." "I respect that", says Opal. "So tell me, what brings you to our 'hood?" Morgan takes a deep breath, and calms herself prior to divulging her story to Opal. "Here goes", stammers Morgan. "I have always had a thing for *'Black Men.'* Since I can remember, Black men have been so fascinating, and they have so much sexy *'swagg'* about them. Their walk is so damn hot to me." "Swagg, huh… you really dig Black men", remarked Opal. "Too make a long story short, I met a man who turned me inside out. He rocked my world as no man ever had. He was so attractive and well put together. This *'White Girl'* lusted for that *"Mandingo"*. I flirted with him until he gave up the *"sausage"*; and boy did he ring my bell

5

over and over, and over again." "I thought he was going to be the one I was going to introduce to my parents. No offense, but they don't believe in inter-racial dating at all." "No offense taken", answers Opal. "Later, I hired a private investigator. Her evidence confirmed my suspicions. He was discovered on numerous occasions "booed-up" with another man. I heard that he was '*Bi-sexual*', and loved his share of 'candy canes.' I wouldn't have believed it until I saw him with a dude named "*Le'Fonz*". A well-known homosexual that has been with attorneys, politicians and damn near everyone else. The man that caused me this heartache was "*Daquan Hightower*" a local, former football great from this town. I'm here Keshia to get a HIV/AIDS test." "Nurse, I have everything to lose here. My Mother is a well-known Neurosurgeon, and my Father a Judge. My husband has his own construction business. All of us live right in the Manhattan region. So you see, discretion is of the utmost importance. I am nothing without my parents, and wealthy husband to finance my lifestyle. I swear to you Nurse, I am a good person... I just got caught up and bored of playin' the desperate housewife, white bread, wholesome, "Soccer Mom" to my 3 kids."

4

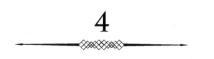

Suddenly, Opal excuses herself; runs to the restroom and proceeds to vomit. Several minutes later, Opal returns to Mrs. Chandler's exam room. "Are you OK? You don't look so hot?" asks Mrs. Chandler. "Yeh thanks. I just had lunch, and I don't think it's agreeing with me.", replies Opal as she vividly, flashbacked to her identical catastrophe with Daquan. "So, if my husband and family try to use their influence to find out about this matter, you must maintain my confidentiality... right?" "Yes that's right; your secret is safe with me," assures Opal. "Before we can continue further, a few more questions," Opal explains. "How long has it been since you had unprotected sex with this Mr. Daquan Hightower, and have you had any other unprotected encounters with other partners?" "It has been four months and counting. Secondly, even my husband uses condoms because he doesn't want anymore children; moreover, I have a gut feeling he thinks I'm cheating on him." "Thank-you for your openness Mrs. Chandler. I'll be back in just a moment." Opal departs gathering a needle, and tubes to draw blood. Opal returns to the exam room. "Are you ready Mrs. Chandler?" "Let's just get this over with", spouts Mrs. Chandler. A few minutes pass. "All done?" "Yes, all done." "I will phone you when the results of the HIV tests are complete. It will take about 2 weeks for the test to arrive back in our office." "Nurse." "Yes." "May I ask for another favor? *I have a secret P.O. Box.* Would you please direct any paper correspondence to this address, and call me on my cell phone at this number bypassing my home phone?" "Sure." Mrs. Chandler hugs Opal, and sheds a tear as she exits. Afterwards, Opal closes the door in utter awe as she is dumbfounded on how much the two actually share in common!

(Opal continues to see patients with diverse infirmities until her shift was over.)

Once arriving back home, Opal eats a light snack; bathes and attempts to melt away her day with slumber. The next morning Opal (now a patient), asks her friend, and Supervisor Sharon to perform the same battery of tests on her, just as she did on a patient the day before. Opal feels embarrassed, and humbled by her pending test results.

5

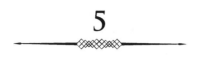

(Weeks pass by.)

(In her efforts to cope, as most folks do in crisis, Opal directs her energies towards GOD for comfort, completion, healing, direction and strength. She quotes Psalm 23, and commits it to memory as most folks in desperation trying to be so spiritual).

"I wonder can I find a descent, God fearing man on a social, dating website", ponders Opal. "On second thought, nawww, I'd better leave that one alone. I'm an ol' fashioned girl. Besides, there are some real perverts/pretenders out there. I should know… I just got seriously burned by one." Opal decides not to sweat a physical relationship, but further her Heavenly relationship with Christ. "In God's time… in God's time." Opal speaks mentally. After many visitations to churches over a several week period, Opal decides upon a quaint, little church nestled on a hilltop. She attends bible study and other services on a reliable basis. Opal now becomes more content with her mission for self-awareness, and her cosmic connection with God.

On the following day at work, Opal contacts Mrs. Chandler by cell as she was instructed… as to maintain Mrs. Chandler's confidence. "Hello. Is this Mrs. Morgan Chandler?" "Yes it is. Is this the Nurse from the clinic?" asks Morgan. "Yes. For security purposes, could you tell me the last four digits of your social and birthdate? Morgan provides the necessary information. "My sincerest apologies that your results arrived later than usual. It seems that our labs are being slammed with these same tests. I have your test results ready, but due to medical policy; we can not provide test results over the phone." "I understand." replies Mrs. Chandler. "May I swing by there this afternoon after work… say around 6ish?" "No problem Mrs. Chandler; I have to stay late this evening to catch up on some charting. I'll see you then." "Ok, thanks so much; see you then." Opal continues to see her appointment patients, and a few 'walk-ins' as well. She decides to skip lunch due to the steady flow of patients.

Six o'clock pm rolls around. No sign of Mrs. Chandler. Several minutes later, Mrs. Chandler arrives at the clinic to see Opal about her HIV/AIDS test. Mrs. Chandler politely apologizes to Opal for being a bit tardy. She explains her "Soccer Mom" duties of picking up her children from their extracurricular activities. Her children amuse themselves at the McDonald's one building over. "Well Ma'am, before I provide the results in which are unknown to myself at this point too; I wanted to have a 'heart to heart'… woman to woman." spoke Opal. Mrs. Chandler nods and becomes jittery.

6

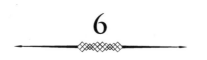

"No matter what these tests indicate, know that God loves you more than you could ever know." Sobbing with all humility, Mrs. Chandler manages to extend her gratitude through the tears. Opal opens the results packet, and warmly grasps Morgan by the hand. "Based on the results, you are clean... there are no antibodies in your system. You're good to go Mrs. Chandler", smiles Opal as she provided the results. "Oh my God, are you kiddin'!? Oh God, Oh God, Oh God... Nurse I can't thank 'you' enough!" gleefully responds Morgan. "Don't thank 'me', thank 'God'." says Opal. "You just don't know what I've been going through. I've been carrying this burden silently from my husband and family. Now, I feel like we have a fighting chance to reconcile! It's as if a huge weight has been lifted; and me forgiven!" "God really does answers prayers; even from people like me who don't deserve it." I can't wait to be the wife I should have been years ago." explains Morgan. "I'm so happy for you Mrs. Chandler.", notes Opal. "If I can serve you in any other possible capacity; please contact me." "I will Nurse... and God Bless You." Mrs. Chandler exits the clinic with handkerchief in hand, and thankfulness of heart. She runs to McDonald's and hugs her children as never before. Afterward, the children look at each other with sheer bewilderment about what just happened.

(Opal wraps up a few more loose ends
at work, and calls it an evening.)

After work, Opal decides to attend a mid-week service at her church. The topic for that evening was… *'Perseverance' and 'Deliverance'*. Opal finds a bit of comfort from the words brought by the Minister. Upon the dismissal of service, Opal notices a new face in the congregation… **and that new face definitely notices her!**

(The following morning Opal heads off to work.
It's a bit slow so Opal and Sharon catch up.)

"So did you go to church last night?" Sharon asks Opal playfully. "Yeh, girl." "So how was it?" "Dish!" "Dang, it was just church girl cool out!" replies Opal. "Hold up. You are up to something Sharon; I know that look anywhere." sharply speaks Opal. "Girl, I don't know what you are talking 'bout." "Oh yeh, ya do!" "Fess up Sharon; I mean it!" Opal responds in frustration. "Ok, ok, ok. There was this dude here last night looking for you after you clocked out. So… I told him how he could find you girl that's all." "Is you crazy! You don't tell a complete stranger how to hunt someone down; he could be freakin' dangerous! What's wrong with you!" remarks Opal in anger. "Hey, I'm sorry. He seemed harmless enough." explains

7

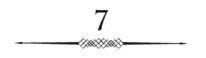

Sharon. "They all appear that way at first." Opal mentions. "Well, did he introduce himself, or talk with you?" "No…, but I did notice a new face last night. He gave me the 'eye' as the service closed." answers Opal. "Did he say what he wanted Sharon when he spoke to you last night?" "No… he just seemed very eager to see you." "Uh, huh. So riddle me this Sharon; Why didn't you try to charm him since you are not in a relationship now yourself?" inquires Opal with obvious doubts of Sharon's true motives. "C'mon now, you my dawg ain't you… anyway, lucky for you Ms. Opal, he was not my type. Otherwise, I would have put the moves on him for myself." "Oh really. So, why wasn't he your type?" Opal asks. "Well, you know. I like 'em *tall, built* and *fine* to da bone!" Not a **'Steve Urkele' lookin' Nigga!**" Sharon responds while snapping her fingers. "Ok… now I see; so it's like that huh? You wanted to set me up with some **'Poindexter', 'bama', 'busta', 'scrub' lookin' Nigga**, and keep all the *fine* brothaz for yourself. What a friend you are Sharon." "Well you know me boo-boo… I gotta keep it real! I'm **'100'** sho nuff!" "I still can't imagine how this guy knows me?" Opal poses. "I'm not sure either, but he show likes what he sees!" laughs Sharon. "Ha ha… real funny!" Opal stammers. "No take backs. He's yours now girlfriend!" Sharon chuckles, and continues to clown on Opal. The two part ways as patients begin to trickle into the office.

(Several days pass. Opal's HIV/
Pregnancy tests finally return.)

"Another day at the rock pile takin' care of sick folks."
Opal sighs to herself. Moments later, Sharon arrives in
the Nurses' locker room, and secretly motions Opal's
attention. Sharon informs Opal that her test results are
in. Opal follows Sharon to a more secluded place in the
building to get the news. "Do you want to do the honors, or
shall I?" asks Sharon. "There ain't nothin' wrong with you
girl. A lot of folks have encounters… so what. It doesn't
mean they pop positive." "I'll do the honors myself. Give me
the envelop Sharon." Opal tears open the sealed envelope,
and proceeds to read the results to herself. "Whew!" says
Kiesha in relief. "See… what did I tell you. You good."
Sharon responds. The two enjoy an elevator ride together,
part ways and proceed to see more patients until closing
time.

(After getting off work, Opal heads home
and proceeds to cry intensely.)

"Oh my God… I can't believe I actually tested positive!"
Opal exclaims while madly pacing back and forth in her
apartment. "I'm too ashamed to tell anyone about this;
especially Sharon. I would never live it down." "My life
is over… what am I gonna do now?" Opal verbalizes
aloud. "Now, I know how some of my patients felt when I
delivered the news to some of them." "I knew I shouldn't
have trusted that Mother****** Daquan after his trifling

ass cheated on me the first time!" "I was a *fool* to get caught up in his looks, and hoopty with 24's!" Opal sobs. "I'm going to kill that titty-squeezin, cock-suckin' 'Son of a Bitch' before the

8

HIV kills us both if it's the last thing I do!" Opal vows mentally. "Forget church!" "I don't give a shit anymore." Opal heads out and purchases a bottle of wine, and a dime bag of weed to cope with her situation. Afterwards, Opal arrives back at her condo and gets high as a kite!

(Opal calls in sick the following morning from her job. She sees Poindexter in the park.)

Opal spends the entire day in the local park in a hypnotic numbness. Later that evening, a stranger sits next to Opal on a bench and introduces himself. "Hello." "You probably don't remember me, but my name is *'Poindexter'*. I met you at my family reunion 2 years ago." Opal stares at Poindexter, and angrily tells him to buzz off. "Please, I mean you no harm." Poindexter responds. "Make it quick then!" Opal states with haste. "As I said, my name is 'Poindexter', and I met you briefly at my family reunion a couple of years back." "That's funny... I sure don't remember meeting you." Opal replies. *"Yeh... I get that a lot."* "You were with my cousin *Daquan Hightower*." Opal turns immediately, and looks at Poindexter with contempt. "Hold up... what did you say?!" said Opal. "Daquan Hightower is my cousin. I was the one who walked into you by accident, and spilled my coleslaw in your lap." "You gotta be kiddin' me right?"

Opal remarks. "No... that was me... two left feet. You and Daquan were so '*booed-up*' together. He has always got the girls since he was an athlete." Poindexter explains with genuine sincerity. "Yeh... now I remember. You messed up my 'club' outfit... I never did get them stains out of my clothes." Opal recalls. "Since that day, I thought you were the prettiest girl I have ever seen. Since Daquan told me he had dumped you... I had to find you. I went to every clinic in the area." "That fool didn't dump me... I'm the one that quit his ass! My friend Sharon told me someone was looking for me not so long ago, and that someone was you?" "Yes. I also saw you in church one night, but I didn't have enough nerve to speak to you." "As you can see... I don't look as handsome as my cousin 'Daquan', but I have a good heart." says Poindexter from the heart. "Why you tellin' me all this?" Opal inquires. "Well... I know something good when I see it. God has given me discernment." "Well, I hate to disappoint you son, but your 'discernment' as you call it, is way off. I'm not good at all. You may need to get your 'radar' fixed!" Opal sharply states. "I don't know what it is, but I know you are dealin' with something heavy currently, and Daquan is probably responsible. "Be of good cheer... God knows and sees your struggle." "Wow... I wonder how he knew something was up with me that Daquan caused. Maybe he does have a sixth sense after all." Opal thinks mentally. "I gotta go." Opal states. "Nice meeting your acquaintance again." states Poindexter as he extends his hand in friendship. "Yeh, OK." Opal responds as she rises to her feet and abruptly departs. "Don't forget... God loves you, and knows your struggle Opal." Poindexter says prior to Opal being out of hearing range. Opal goes home, and attempts to process the unique episode that she just encountered.

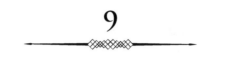

9

(Opal goes to work the next morning still contemplating her condition and encounter.)

Opal remains busy throughout the morning attending to patients. She decides to re-visit the park for her lunch break. Opal decides not to invite Sharon so that she could digest her recent health scare. While there, she eats a light meal and feeds the ducks. Opal ponders retribution/revenge on Daquan for infecting her with HIV. Afterwards, Opal returns to work. "Hey girl, where you been?" inquires Sharon feeling like she was just jilted. "Just coming back from lunch," responds Opal. "Girl… you are actin' some kinda funny. Something wrong?" inquires Sharon. "Just got a lot on my mind that's all. Is that OK with you?" replies Opal sharply. "No need to bite my head off child; besides, I have to show you something that may cheer you up." Sharon escorts Opal to her work station. "Tadaaaa… you got *'flowers* delivered to you; *'a dozen red roses'* as matter of fact!" "What did you do Sharon… count 'em?!" "Yeh girl, you know how I do." Opal pauses for a moment not knowing what to think. "Well… what are you waiting for? Who are they from?" Sharon impatiently asks. Opal slowly removes the card from the mini envelope pinned to the flowers. "They're from *'Poindexter'*. "Poindexter… who da hell is Poindexter?" "Well, if you must know, he was the dude that came looking for me here that day. Remember?"

responds Opal. "I saw him yesterday in the park; well better yet, *he spotted me* in the park." "Oh yeh, that **'boo-boo', 'scrub'** lookin' Nigga! Ya'll got a thang for each other now? You've been creepin' and holdin' out on me Opal." "No Sharon… slow your roll, and get your mind outta the gutter." "He's Daquan's cousin. I recalled meeting him at Daquan's family reunion not so long ago. Nothing more, nothing less." With some doubt Sharon responds back. "Ok… I hear ya." "He ain't that much to look at is he Opal?" poses Sharon. "He's not as fine as Daquan no doubt, but he ain't that bad." "You go head on stuff… defend your **'new man'**!" "He ain't my man!" Opal states with anger. Sharon continues to clown on Sharon as she goes back down the hallway. Sharon concludes by informing Opal about the pending inventory of the Medical Lab. The day continues with Opal worrying about her HIV positive status that she contracted from Daquan. Even with all that mind-bending, stomach-twisting stress, she occasionally glances at her flowers, and her brief encounter with Poindexter. Working like an empty shell, Opal muddles her way through the numerous ailments of her patients. Later, she clocks out, and makes a detour prior to heading home.

10

(Opal seeks to purchase a gun.)

Opal canvasses the 'hood' hoping to find an inexpensive gun. It's a warm day, and Opal begins to sweat while she is pounding the pavement. She removes her lab jacket and name tag. Perspiration is glistening between her bosom. She is approached by "Sweets", a well-known pimp with women, money and a bad attitude to match. "Hey foxy thang... what's your name?" inquires Sweets to Opal. "My name is *'Mind your own damn business', or you can call me 'Puddintang'*!' exclaims Opal. "Ok Momma; you ain't got to bite a brothaz head off.", responds Sweets as he tries to 'mac' and 'swagg'. "Whooooweee... you are sure put together mighty fine Momma! Suppose I offer you a job working with ol' Sweets. Would ya like that?" Opal stares at Sweets with bulging eyes. "Hell No... I don't roll like that! What you could do since you are in the business of helpin' people and all, is to tell me where I can buy a clean gun. How 'bout that?!" Sweets takes a moment to contemplate Opal's request while he 'licks his lips'. As Sweets leans at an angle trying to 'profile', he replies to Opal's question. "Alright baby girl... don't let it be known that Ol' Sweets here don't help da ladies in distress. Just keep walking until you come to 'Mookies House of Chicken and Ribs'. Ask for 'Monroe'... he's a hustlin', *'crackhead'* that would sell his **own Momma** for a fix!" "Hell... his sister is turnin' tricks for me right now! Just tell Monroe that 'Sweets' sent ya. He'll look out for you." "Yeh… thanks. You've done your good deed for the day." answers Opal. The company part ways. While walking in the opposite direction, Sweets turns his head to get another glimpse of Opal with free enterprise on his mind.

(Opal enters "Mookies House of Chicken and Ribs.")

Opal eyeballs the joint for a moment. Folks inside stare her down like she is a fish out of water… or that she could be 'Po-Po'. After a moment and leaving the grill, Mookie approaches Opal and says… "Can I help you Miss?" "I'm lookin' Monroe. Sweets sent me. Is he here?" "Sweets sent you huh?" Mookie pauses looking Opal up and down as to get a sense that she is not the police. "Yeh, he's here. Just walk through my back exit into the alley. Monroe and some more homeboys are back there shootin' craps. Monroe is the skinniest Nigga out there; you can't miss him." "Bet.", Opal remarks, and nods at Mookie. Mookie returns to the grill secretly holding his crotch. Opal reaches the back of the restaurant, and motions in Monroe's direction. He tells her to wait while he shoots the dice. "Seven again Niggaz… pay me; I'm

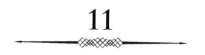
gonna take all y'all 'rent money' you broke ass Mother*******!" laughs Monroe as he collects his winnings. 'Scuze me, while I go chat with this Philly that needs Monroe's attention.

As Monroe comes to his feet from kneeling, one of the guys says… "Don't laugh too hard; you'll be givin' me my own money back in a few hours when your *'junky ass'* begs to buy this *'grape sized crack rock'* for a 'fix' I got in my pocket!" The rest of the guys laugh in hysterics! Monroe gives the group the 'finger' as he approaches Opal. "What can Monroe do for you Shorty?" "I need a gun. Sweets said you would look out for me.", Opal replies. "So Sweets sent me some business… a nice 'lookin' piece of business too." "Can you help me or not… it's getting' late." Opal mentions. "Step over here Shorty." "Let Monroe show his *'gun'*". Monroe makes a proposition to Opal while unzipping his pants. "If you *'blow my gun'*, I'll *give* you a gun." The guys stop their play to see how Opal reacts to Monroe's proposition. "I tell you what Man, I'll give you my grandfather's *'switchblade'* in my purse through your *'cocktail weeny'*… how 'bout that!", bluffs Opal with manufactured bravado. The guys burst out in laughter yet again! "Whoa… no need for violence Sugar! Monroe was just playin' that all." Monroe reaches down in his right sock, and pulls out a gorgeous .22 caliber. "125 dollars and it's yours." "Is it clean?" asks Opal. Monroe begins to show

Opal the gun. "No serial numbers… fresh from Mexico." "Here's 100 dollars… now give me *my* gun!" "Damn! You sure are a tough cookie! Alright, I'll take it." Opal gives Monroe the 100 dollar bill, and reaches back in her purse to grab a *'latex glove'*. "What with the glove honey? I told you the gun was clean didn't I?" "It ain't that *'clean'*… I saw where it came from with your *'ashy', 'rusty' ankles!* Opal snatches the gun and proceeds to saunter away. The guys trip out laughing more due to how Opal clowned/joked out Monroe!

(Opal later arrives back home.)

"Whew… what a day! I am so exhausted." Opal collapses in her recliner for a few moments, and plots her revenge on the man that infected her with 'HIV'. She begins to fondle the gun as to relay intent. "I'd better go in here now and take a long, hot bath to clean this 'funk' off me before I start nodding.", remarks Opal aloud. Opal goes to the refrigerator, and pours herself a glass of chilled wine; she then proceeds to her bathroom. She begins to run her bath water as hot as she can stand it… adds her favorite bath wash …. turns on some 'jazz', and slowly begins to 'exhale' after the water envelopes her with love, warm caresses. The sipping of her fine wine further intoxicates her relaxation. Prior to retiring for the night, Opal makes herself a pimento cheese sandwich accompanied by Vanilla wafers; she goes down for the count.

12

(Inventory at the Clinic. Opal confides to Sharon.)

Opal comes in to work a bit tardy. Sharon stands in the lobby tapping her feet, and pointing at her watch. "Don't start Sharon, I'm not in the mood", states Opal. "Hey, don't you trip either "Miss Thang", we have to do inventory on medical supplies today." "Luckily, the clinic will be closing several hours earlier today so we can get this done." "Ok, Sharon I hear ya." "Girl, you and I are going to have a 'heart to heart' talk while we do inventory. Something is going on with you that you are hiding... I can feel it", responds Sharon. Opal lowers her head, and proceeds to call her first patient. Later, once the clinic closes, Sharon seeks out Opal. The two begin to scan medical supplies for inventory. After about 30 minutes of silence between the two, Sharon tells Opal to 'dish'. "Look Opal, I know I rag on you sometimes, but you know you are my girl right?" "What is up with you lately... you have been edgy and uptight." Opal stares at Sharon as if she could drop her with a right punch, but decides to disclose to Sharon instead. "Understand this here Sharon... what I am 'bout to tell you is strictly between you and I only... absolutely no one else... you feel me!" "If it gets out, I know you told it, and I will never ever speak to you again, and I will lie to deny your accusation. You got me good before I go any further?!" "I swear I won't tell another Soul Opal as long as I live." "You better not." Opal and Sharon go into a back area of the medical supply room. They both look around carefully to insure there is no one else present. The coast was clear. Opal takes a deep sigh. "I do have a confession to make Sharon". Opal takes in a deep, cleansing breath.

"You recall the HIV test I had after messin' around with Daquan right?" "Yeh, what of it … you told me you tested clean right?" Opal lowers her head and sobs. Sharon pieces it together by Opal's crying. "No… No… it can't be… Opal don't play with me like this… this shit ain't funny." replies Sharon in total disbelief. "It's, It's true Sharon… I tested positive for HIV." "Sharon embraces Opal, and the duo have a sisterly type moment. "Opal, what in the hell happened?" "You know when you gave me the HIV test initially; I told you Daquan was gay when I caught him in the bed with another man." "Damn… I just don't know what to say Opal". "I do know that I am here for you in whatever way possible." "Thanks Sharon". "I got to handle my business tonight." "Gotta get some revenge on that Nigga Daquan." "What are you sayin' girl?" Sharon questions. "Don't worry 'bout me I got this; worry about that fool Daquan." "Opal… you are really scaring me now!" replies Sharon. "Don't be scared… just keep your word about not blabbing my business." "Ok… but please Opal, promise me you won't do

13

anything stupid." Opal does not respond back to Sharon's plea. Instead she continues to tally inventory in the lab. Sharon touches Opal on the shoulder and continues the job at hand.

(Inventory is completed.)

"Thank God that's over", Sharon responds. "I don't want to hear anything about God right now", remarks Opal sharply. "He ain't thinking 'bout me, and I sure ain't thinking 'bout Him." "Opal, I know I use profanity, but I revere God in my own way. I am praying that He delivers me from some things." "Don't get to the point of no return and blaspheme. Even I know better than that." Sharon states to correct Opal. "I gotta go." "Got to put in some work!" "Opal I beg you don't leave here, and do something stupid. Tell ya what, why don't you come to my place, and we can have a 'girls' night." "No thanks", Opal states as she grabs her purse. "Opal... please don't do this". "Holla back", Opal replies. Opal exits and doesn't look back. As by fate, moments later, Poindexter arrives at the clinic searching for Opal. He runs into Sharon. "Excuse me, my name is Poindexter. Could you please tell me where Opal is? "God must have sent you". "What's going on? Why would you say that?" states Poindexter as he becomes stressed. "You got to go after Opal!" "I think she is going to kill your cousin Daquan!" "What!", exclaims Poindexter in total despair. "What would cause Opal to contemplate such a thing?!" questions Poindexter. "There's no time for this! Please go after Opal at Daquan's and hurry!" Poindexter darts out of the clinic, and heads to Daquan's apartment.

(The Confrontation.)

"I can't wait to see the expression on Daquan's face when I threaten to kill his ass." Opal ponders as she reaches Daquan's complex. Poindexter too is in hot pursuit. He prays *"The Lord's Prayer"* for everyone's protection who's involved. A few minutes later, he also arrives at Daquan's place. Opal gains entrance to Daquan's apartment. She remembered she made a duplicate copy of Daquan's door key when they first met. She fumbles for her door key while trying to get her composure. Finally, Opal stealthily enters Daquan's. She closes the door somewhat; not knowing it's slightly ajar. Opal enters the living room while tip-toeing around. She has a clear view of the Kitchen from the living room. She does not see Daquan, but hears voices come from the bathroom. Opal slowly creeps towards the bathroom door. She hears giggling, and what sounds like *"sexual pleasures"*. Now being so outraged, Opal slams the door open; pulls back the shower curtain, and sees her cousin Meeka, Le'Fonz (Daquan's gay lover), and Daquan having a *"Threesome"*! The trio are shocked to the core, and immediately tell Opal to

14

"get the hell out", wondering what she was even doing there. "Meeka… I can't believe you… you did this shit to me one time before with Daquan… and I forgave your Black ass! "He's fair game now, I know you and Daquan broke up a while back!" Meeka yells. "Yeh Bitch, take your 'no man havin' ass' up out of here!" Le'Fonz remarks as he strokes Daquan's wet genitals.

"Meeka you're a damn fool to 'lay up' with a gay man!" yells Opal. "He's got enough *"Dick"* to share!" says Meeka as she tugs Daquan's penis. *Not being able to take anymore grief, Opal pulls out her gun! "I came here to kill Daquan's ass, but now I can send all 3 of you Fuckers straight to Hell where you belong!"* Daquan, Le'Fonz and Meeka begin to fear for their lives as Opal holds them hostage! All three of them beg and plead to Opal not to kill them! Their pleas are all in vain! Opal cocks the gun, and aims at the sinful trio! From out of nowhere, Poindexter rushes in, and confronts Opal! "Opal, Opal… please put the gun down!" asks Poindexter. "I know you are hurting, but this is not worth it". "Killing them is only going to make all your problems worse." "Please, Please give me the gun." Opal shakes with the gun in hand; while Daquan, Le'Fonz and Meeka tremble covering themselves up with towels! Opal begins to cry, and gives the gun to Poindexter. Poindexter leads Opal out of Daquan's apartment to his car. He grasps Opal's hand to console her anguish. Poindexter drives

Opal back to her place. He makes a detour down a dirt road to throw Opal's gun into the local river.

(Poindexter and Opal confide in each other.)

"I don't know exactly what Daquan did to you, but witnessing what I saw earlier, and knowing my cousin; it can't be good." "You just don't know how that man has changed my life forever", stutters Opal. "Well… I have a secret too Opal", mentions Poindexter. "If I trust you with my secret… will you trust me with yours?" Opal feels a sense of 'Peace', 'Comfort' and 'Integrity' with Poindexter. So, she nods her head in agreement. Nervously, Poindexter begins to speak. "Well, um… well… uh… umm…" "Just go ahead Poindexter… I won't judge or laugh at you", promises Opal. "Ok… well Opal… I know this will sound strange, but *I am a Virgin.*" Opal pauses for a moment. Poindexter holds his head down with some embarrassment. Opal replies… "You are a one-of-a-kind". "I wish I could say that I was a virgin after all the crap I've been through." Poindexter raises his head in relief. "You are the first person I have ever told", remarks Poindexter. "I've always been fond of you since I met you at the cookout a while back with Daquan." "You being so beautiful… I was just infatuated with my cousin's girlfriend." Opal now speaks to Poindexter. "I don't know what I am going to do, but I am completely devastated by what I'm about to say." *"I discovered that I am HIV positive."* Poindexter slowly rises to his feet. He reaches out his arms to hug Opal. Opal now stands, embracing Poindexter

15

while sobbing on his shoulder. The couple share a moment. "I can't imagine how you must feel", Poindexter tells Opal. *"This may sound strange to you, but I know someone that can cure you of this disease completely and forever."* Opal looks at Poindexter with doubt and resentment. "How could you say such a thing to me?!" I am in the Medical Field... I treat 'STD' patients all the time; there's no cure for HIV!" exclaims Opal.

(Poindexter tells Opal to come with him somewhere.)

The church where Poindexter saw Opal was having their final night of church revival. The theme for the revival is *"Miracles."* Opal rides with Poindexter unknowing the destination. Once they arrive, Opal becomes suspicious and skeptical. "Please trust me", beckons Poindexter. Opal reluctantly enters the sanctuary with Poindexter. The service has nearly ended. The Pastor tells the congregation that... *"Nothing is too hard, or impossible for God."* The Pastor asks for persons that are burdened/in bondage to come at the altar. He further reminds them that *"God is able."* Poindexter looks at Opal. He motions for Opal to go to the altar. He further states that she does not have to divulge her secret; because God already knows. Opal feels a bit shy about approaching the altar. She notices others in the congregation walking towards the altar in expectation.

Several men approach the altar weeping. Suddenly, Opal rises to her feet as if she was guided by a kind spirit. She too goes to the altar weeping.

(The Masses arrive at the Altar.)

The Pastor opens his Bible and reads from Romans, Chapter 10, verses 9-10. *"That if thou confess with thy mouth The Lord Jesus, and shall believe in thine heart that God raised Him from the dead, thou shall be saved. For with the heart believeth unto righteousness; and with the mouth confession is made unto salvation.* All those present at the altar have been moved by The Holy Scriptures. Each seeks to be saved. The Pastor motions to his Deacons to provide the "Anointing Oil". Once anointed, a few casually return to their seats. A few more remain at the altar waving their hands, and leaping for joy! Opal is most moved at the altar. *After receiving Salvation, Opal falls to her knees, and asks God for Forgiveness of her sins. She prays silently for a "Miraculous Supernatural Healing" of her HIV disease. Opal departs from the altar praising God in the Highest! Poindexter becomes filled with the goodness of the Lord, and begins to shout "Glory".* Once church was dismissed, the Pastor was led by the Lord to approach Opal. He hugs her intensely and remarked... "I don't know what you prayed for,

16

but remember... **'God is able.'**" Opal returned the hug to the Pastor. The Congregation is dismissed. Some linger in the church parking lot still rejoicing! Poindexter drives Opal back to her apartment. He again grasps her hand prior to her exiting the car. Poindexter tells Opal to keep the faith as she waved goodnight.

(The following morning, Opal heads
to work feeling renewed.)

Due to the large patient load, Sharon does not see Opal until lunchtime. Sharon has been worrying about her friend all night. Later, during lunch, Sharon notices Opal seated reading a small, olive green book. It turned out to be a New Testament Bible that she received from church the night before. "Girl, I have been worrying about you all night... What happened...? What went down?", "Sharon inquires. Opal sighs. "Well... I nearly did something stupid. I went to Daquan's apartment to kill him for what he done to me. When I arrived, his gay lover Le'Fonz was there; and my cousin Meeka that he cheated on me with before. They were having a threesome." "That's some wild ****! Your cousin Meeka is sick in the head... a real 'freakazoid'", replies Sharon. "I can only imagine what went through your mind Opal when you saw what you did." "I know girl. Fortunately for me, Poindexter arrived moments before I was going to pull the trigger. I wonder how he found out where I was?" Sharon stammers. "Well... um... you see..." "Don't fret Sharon... I ain't mad with you... For once, I am glad you did not keep your word." "So Opal... you are still holdin' something back. What happened after you and Poindexter left Daquan's apartment? Did y'all do da 'Nasty'?" "Get your mind out of the gutter... can't you think about anything else?" "I'm just asking?" Sharon coyly remarks.

"No... Poindexter was a perfect gentleman... he actually took me to church." "He took you where?" Sharon says in astonishment. "Yes... he took me to church. A *"Miraculous"/"Marvelous"* event happened." "What girl... did he propose to you at the church house?" "No Sharon... not only did I get *"Saved"*, but I also got a *"Miracle"!"* "What kind of miracle exactly are you talkin' 'bout Opal?" *"I know that God has healed me from the HIV virus."* "Say what?!" Sharon remarks with sharp criticism. *"I know God is able Sharon... no matter what you, or anyone else may think. I felt Him purge my body from HIV... I know, that I know that I know... and you can't make me believe otherwise."* "Ok 'boo-boo'... don't bite my head off." "You don't believe me do you Sharon?" "I didn't say that." "No you don't have to... I know what you are doubting." "Tell you what... go to the medical supply bin, and get

17

some of my blood for another HIV test." "Are you sure you want to do this Opal?" "Positive." Sharon does as Opal request, and gets another sample of blood for the test." Once completed, the vile was sent to the lab with a "rush status". Sharon and Opal get back to work after Opal's blood was drawn.

(The Conclusion)

Days pass. The medical courier arrives at the clinic with Opal's results. Sharon is on pins and needles, but Opal does not seem pressed. Sharon snatches the sealed results from Opal before she opens it. As Sharon tears into the envelop and begins to read... her eyes bulge! "Well... I'll be damned... I just can't believe this", responds Sharon. Opal stares at Sharon. Sharon nearly loses her balance after reading the results! Sharon attempts to regain her composure. "If I didn't see this for myself, I would've have never believed it." ***"Opal, your HIV results are Negative!"*** "See... I told you." ***"GOD IS ABLE... THERE'S NOTHING TOO HARD FOR GOD".*** Still in awe, Sharon gives the results letter to Opal, and heads for the breakroom to absorb what just happened. Opal heads back to the lobby to call her last patient of the day... Lo, and behold; it's "Mrs. Morgan Chandler". She was the woman who messed around too with Daquan. Opal had given her an HIV test which came back clean. Opal remembers the prior plight of Mrs. Chandler. Opal asks what brings Mrs. Chandler back to the office since she was not infected. "Mrs. Morgan... a pleasure to see you... you look good too." "Call me Morgan". "Yes... things are getting better with my husband and I since my infidelity. He has forgiven me. My family and I are now looking for a "Church Home".

"Well, my boyfriend Poindexter and I know just the place..."

Sharon later joins the fold too, and gives her life to Christ.

THE END.

One more page to read... turn over.

***EMAIL ME... I WOULD LOVE
TO HEAR FROM YOU!

emailmeog@yahoo.com

***PLEASE CHECK OUT MY OTHER BOOKS.

THIS HAS BEEN A "4.0
GPA – AUTHOR" GEM

Printed in the United States
by Baker & Taylor Publisher Services